WREN

WOLVES OF THE RISING SUN #7

KENZIE COX

Published by Bayou Moon Press, LLC, 2015.

This is a work of fiction. Similarities to real people, places, or events are entirely coincidental.

Wren: WOLVES OF THE RISING SUN #7
First edition.

Copyright © 2015 Kenzie Cox.
Written by Kenzie Cox.

Join the Packs of the Mating Season

The mating moon is rising...

Wherever that silver light touches, lone male werewolves are seized by the urge to find their mates. Join these six packs of growly alpha males (with six-packs!) as they seek out the smart, sassy women who are strong enough to claim them forever.

The "Mating Season" werewolf shifter novellas are brought to you by six authors following the adventures of six different packs. Each novella is the story of a mated pair (or trio!) with their Happily Ever After. Enjoy the run!

Learn more at thematingseason.com

Wren: Wolves of the Rising Sun

His wolf can't forget her…

Wren Davenne can't forget those two nights he spent with his raven-haired beauty. And now, after going MIA for over two weeks, Bella Stone is suddenly back in his life. Only she's all business, while he's all play… mostly. But when her life is threatened, the games are off and he'll stop at nothing to save her.

Bella Stone has a past. An ugly one. But she's put that all behind her and joined the FBI. And now she has a job to do… even if she keeps getting distracted by the wolf Wren Davenne. But when her current case and her past collide, there's a lot more than her job on the line. She's going to have to endure the fight of her life is she wants to survive and find her happily-ever-after.

Sign up for Kenzie's newsletter here at www.kenziecox.com. Do you prefer text messages? Sign up for text alerts! Just text SHIFTERSROCK to 24587 to register.

CHAPTER 1
BELLA

Ryker Jamison. Just uttering his name was enough to make people stop and give you their undivided attention. After a week of trying to hunt down information on my fellow FBI agent, Fischer, and his possible involvement in a human trafficking ring, every single lead had sent me straight to Ryker's front door.

Or to be more accurate, his dragon lair disguised as a motorcycle shop.

Ryker Jamison was the leader of the Dragons of Decatur, the unofficial Robin Hood of

New Orleans. According to all my Intel, the dragon shifters were the ones to go to if someone needed anything done in this town. And I do mean everything: permits for buildings, untangling legal issues, information, muscle for hire, and just about anything else one could think of. They were fixers, and despite not being part of the civic government, the ones who ran the city.

The large tattooed man sat behind the desk, his hands clasped behind his head as he stared at me. "So, what brings you to my corner of the world, Ms. Stone?"

I leaned forward. "I need information, and I'm told you're the guy to ask."

His gaze dropped to my cleavage and when I glanced down, I bit back a curse. Son of a… the top button had popped on my blouse. The edge of my black lace bra along with plenty of flesh was on full display. I sat back and tugged at my shirt, trying for some sort of decency. "Excuse me," I said. "This is not how I normally conduct business."

He gave me a slow smile. "I'm willing to step outside the lines."

"I'm not," I said sharply and passed him a picture of Fischer I'd gotten from his file. "Have you seen this man?"

Without looking at the picture he asked, "Why?"

I kept my expression neutral. "I need to talk to him."

Ryker raised one eyebrow, piercing me with his stare. "That seems obvious. You're going to need to do better than that if you want my help."

I gritted my teeth. The dragon was a dealer of information. He wasn't going to help me unless I gave him something useful. "I have reason to believe he may be part of a human trafficking ring."

"I see." He held my gaze for another beat and then glanced down at the picture. He studied it for a moment, then slid it back across the desk. "Sorry. Haven't seen him."

Tucking the picture back into my bag, I frowned. "That's it? Haven't seen him? Have you heard about the abductions? Everyone I've spoken to says you're the guy with his thumb on the pulse of the city. You don't have anything else?"

His other eyebrow rose. "And why would I tell you if I did," he glanced down at a piece of paper in front of him, "Bella?"

"Because I'm trying to work an investigation."

"FBI?" he asked, interest finally creeping into his tone.

"Yes, and I'd appreciate your cooperation. Working together we could—"

He held up his hand. "I don't work with anyone in a position of authority. In this town it's the quickest way to get burned. If you know anything about New Orleans, you know that no one is who they say or seem to be. You can understand my hesitation. Trust has to be earned around here."

"I'm not from here," I shot back. "I'm from Knoxville, TN. We're a little more on the straight and narrow up there."

His lips curved into a sardonic smile. "I've heard Fischer is from Nashville. If he's a suspect, it doesn't paint a picture of trustworthiness, now does it?"

I stared into his deep dark eyes and knew I wasn't going to get anywhere today. He obviously knew who Fischer was, but he was going to dig into my background first before he'd supply me with even a hint of information. I crossed my arms over my chest. "How long will it take you?"

He narrowed his eyes. "Take me to do what?"

"Run a check on me. It doesn't take a genius to realize you don't deal with anyone you don't know inside and out. Well," I stood and threw my card down on his desk, "let me save you some trouble. I'm FBI agent Isabella Stone, been with the Bureau for three years, worked the desk for two, started in the field nine months ago. I've closed four of five cases. Fischer is number five. I graduated from an ivy league when I was twenty-one, have a sealed juvenile record, and both my parents are in prison."

At my last admission, he straightened and peered at me. "Your parents are incarcerated? What for?"

"Fraud." When he just nodded, I added, "You're not interested in my record?"

He sat back in his chair and gave me a small smile. "I'd rather be surprised."

"I see," I said, careful to keep a neutral tone. Letting on just how irritated I was wasn't going to help anyone. "In the meantime, women in your city are in danger. And if you're holding back information, you'll have that on your conscience." Without waiting for a response, I got up and headed for the door.

CHAPTER 2

WREN

The Harley rumbled with perfect precision beneath me, the performance a product of my brother Darien's handiwork. I sped up, darting in and out of the French Quarter traffic until I swung into the Dragons of Decatur bike shop.

"Sweet ride," Gabe, one of the mechanics, said over the roar of the engine. He was dressed in torn jeans and a black T-shirt, the shop's usual uniform.

I killed the engine and climbed off. "Too

bad it belongs to that asshole, Chase. A beast this nice deserves an owner who isn't a douche."

Gabe grinned wryly and tucked a greasy rag in the back pocket of his jeans. "His money's good though."

"Not with Darien." I handed him the key. "He doesn't want shit from Chase. Probably has something to do with that broken nose Darien gave him last week."

Gabe's brows rose in question. "Something I should know about?"

I shook my head. "Nothing important. Chase insulted Darien's girl. Darien clocked him. Now I'm delivering the bike here so the two don't have to see each other ever again."

"Got it." Gabe pocketed the keys. "I'll make sure he gets it."

"Thanks." I pointed to the back office. "Is Ryker in? We have an appointment."

The tall man nodded. "He's in his office. Said to send you back when you got here."

"Thanks."

"No problem." Gabe cast the Harley one last look, then went back to work on the custom chopper currently taking up the majority of the bay.

I made my way into the back, admiring the impeccably clean shop. Every tool was stored away, the floor and counters spotless, and not a speck of dust anywhere. The place looked like it could rival my kitchen in cleanliness.

There was only one office in the shop, and the wooden door was closed. It had the Dragons of Decatur emblem burned into the wood along with Ryker's name beneath it. Just Ryker.

No last name. He didn't need one.

Everyone knew Ryker, leader of the dragon shifters.

Ryker was a fixer, always sidestepping the law for the greater good. How he got away with it, no one knew. There was speculation he had dirt on the city leaders and used it to his advantage. However he did it, I didn't care. Today all I wanted was information on Shade, aka, FBI Agent Fischer.

I raised my hand to knock, but the door swung open, revealing a gorgeous raven beauty.

She let out a surprised gasp, blinked, and then took one step back as if I'd just invaded her personal space. "Wren? What are you doing here?"

"Bella?" My gaze went straight to her ample cleavage spilling out of her silk top.

"Um," she glanced down, following my gaze and grimaced as her cheeks flushed pink. "I was just—"

"You don't need to explain." Though my wolf rose to the surface, ready to demand answers. Just last week, she'd been in my bed. Been *mine*. And now here she was in Ryker's office doing god knows what.

"Right." She pulled her jacket closed, covering herself as the pink staining her cheeks brightened. "Well, it was good to see you."

"You, too." I watched her walk down the hall and disappear into the garage bay.

"Wren." Ryker's raspy voice filtered from the office.

I tore my eyes away from the door, fighting the instinct to go after her. Dammit. She wasn't mine. Not even close. We'd had two nights together before she'd disappeared on me. Then last week she'd shown up at the Hidden Bayou Resort I owned with my brothers, flashing her FBI badge.

"What was she doing here?" I asked the dragon as I sat across from him.

"Why? What's it to you?" Ryker never answered questions without payment. In this case it was clear he wanted information, not cash.

Fair enough. "She's investigating the case I'm here to talk to you about. It's quite the coincidence we both turned up at the same time. Was she buying or selling?"

He chuckled. "From the looks of her, I'd say she was definitely selling something."

I let out a low growl, unable to control my reaction.

His chuckle turned to a laugh. "Relax, wolf.

I was joking. She was here looking for information."

"But?"

He shrugged. "I don't know her, so she didn't get anywhere. What do you have on her?"

"Nothing. She's FBI. That's all I know."

"That's not what I hear." His lips spread into a knowing smile, but the suspicion lurking in his eyes said he wasn't as amused as he pretended to be.

Jesus. Nothing was sacred. I wasn't about to tell him I knew about the tattoo on her hip or the faint birthmark on her upper thigh. "Been keeping tabs on me, Ryker? Or her?"

He pressed his lips together in a thin line. After a moment, he said, "Her. But if it looks like you're keeping information from me, I won't hesitate to put one of my guys on you."

My blood started to boil and my wolf stirred, ready to pounce. I took a deep breath and ignored the urge, reminding myself there was a reason we could always count on him for information. He never overlooked anything. "Listen, I don't talk about my personal life with anyone. Ever. All I'll say is that we spent a couple of nights together before I knew she was FBI. Judging by her surprise last week when we ran into each other at the resort, I'm guessing she had no idea I was part of the pack that was right in the middle of this case. Considering you've been keeping tabs on her, I'm betting you know more about her than I do."

"Possibly." He rubbed his jaw. "But nothing as intimate as you've managed to discover."

"Ryker," I growled.

He shook his head in amusement. "You wolves are all the same. So emotional. Get it under control. I have no interest in your FBI agent past what she knows about this so-called human trafficking ring."

"So-called? You don't think it actually exists?" I asked.

He shrugged. "Doubtful." The middle drawer of his desk squeaked as he pulled it open. A second later, he produced a thick cardstock envelope and slid it across the metal desk.

I took the cream envelope and without opening it, I asked, "Are you seriously saying you're ignoring the fact that someone in your town is abducting women?"

His green eyes darkened and his muscles bunched as he clenched his fists and leaned forward, piercing me with his penetrating stare. His gaze was so intense, I swore I saw a fire burning there. "I'll let that one pass just this once, Davenne. But if you question my integrity again, we're going to have a problem."

"Relax," I said, holding my ground, glad to see I hit a nerve. I was starting to wonder if he'd brushed the accusations off. "I'm just curious why this doesn't seem to be a priority for you. Is there something deeper going on we don't know about?"

He rolled his shoulders and let out a long breath. "I never said I didn't think someone was abducting women. Just that I have my suspicions about it being a trafficking ring. It's my belief the women are being taken for a different purpose, pornography perhaps. We're not certain they're being sold. There are implications this case is tied to a major player in our city and that's my main focus at the moment." He pointed at the envelope. "I gave you that evidence because I want you to track down the street boss while I deal with the bigger fish. Got it?"

I sat back in the chair and rested my foot on my knee, relaxing for the first time since I'd entered his lair. "Yeah, man. I got it. Sorry about the mix up. It's just that two of our newest members to the pack were targets and this is personal."

"Understood." He nodded to the letter. "You gonna open that?"

I pulled the note out of the envelope and scanned the invitation twice. Then I read it out loud.

Exclusive, invitation only, silent auction. Saturday at 4 p.m. Location: Algiers Point. The Warehouse.

"What are they auctioning?" I asked Ryker.

His voice was low and full of rage when he answered. "Turn it over."

I flipped the invitation and read the inscription, *Charlie's Little Darlings.*

"Son of a bitch! I thought that bastard was behind bars." Charlie of Charlie's Little Darlings was a sex club owner who'd been put away in the state pen after being convicted of multiple counts of forced prostitution, drug trafficking, and homicide. He was a stain on the city, and once he'd been put away, crime had gone down ten percent overnight. The auction would be for "art" photos of the women who worked for him.

"He is. But it appears he has a new associate. Someone by the name of Fischer."

CHAPTER 3

BELLA

I SAT AT the cafe directly across from the bike shop, ignoring the cappuccino I'd ordered. The last thing I needed after running into Wren was more caffeine, but ordering decaf was a crime against nature. No self respecting FBI agent would be caught with unleaded fuel in her veins.

It'd been twenty minutes since I'd left the garage, and my heart rate was still elevated. How could just the sight of a man turn me into a jittery mess? I needed to snap out of it. Fast.

He had not been part of the plan.

Two weeks ago, I'd run into him at a trendy bar in the Arts District. One thing had led to another and we'd ended up at a hotel for the night. Two nights later, I'd accidentally-on-purpose run into him at his restaurant. And well…we'd ended up back at that same hotel.

Wren Davenne was the worst kind of distraction. One that, if I let myself, I could end up losing myself in. That was unacceptable. Lives were on the line and mistakes could be deadly. And since I wasn't in New Orleans to find a boyfriend, and I had a job to do, I'd ruthlessly cut myself off from the one man who'd ever managed to get under my skin. That is until last week when he'd landed right in the middle of my investigation. Now I had no choice but to deal with him.

Especially since it looked like he'd get more information out of the dragon than I had. They knew each other, had history, while I was the new girl with no trust. I hadn't expected Ryker to open up with me right off. I knew there'd be a waiting period before I got anything out of him, but now there was Wren. And one way or another, before the day was over, I'd find out why Wren was meeting with Ryker.

"Anything else for you, ma'am?" the young waiter asked, blocking my view of the bike shop.

"No. Thank you. Just the check." I craned my neck, only to be thwarted by a group of gutter punks milling around on the sidewalk, the four of them sharing a forty-ounce beer.

"Are you sure? Today's bread pudding is off the charts. And we have Crème brûlée as well as flourless chocolate cake. Any one of those would be the perfect complement to—"

"Just the check," I snapped and stood up, catching sight of Wren as he strode down the street, disappearing into the middle of a crowd. "Dammit." I threw a twenty down on the table. "Never mind. That should cover it."

"But—"

I took off, running in my high heels, and prayed I didn't fall and break my neck. The uneven streets and sidewalks may have been more dangerous than the last shootout I'd engaged in. At least then the chance of breaking an ankle had been minimal.

"Excuse me." I pushed past a tourist wearing the skimpiest black tank top paired with shorts so short, her ass cheeks hung out. But she'd classed the outfit up with a pair of lace-up leather boots and a purple feather boa.

"Watch it," the tourist said.

"Sorry!" I grimaced and quickened my pace. Son of a…I'd lost him. The sidewalk was clear in front of me save a dog curled up in front of a small art gallery. No Wren anywhere.

I slowed to a brisk walk, peering into each of the storefronts, wondering if he'd stopped for something.

But then, just as I walked past the sleeping dog, a hand reached out from behind a pillar and grabbed my arm.

"What the hell?" I jumped and tried to wrench my arm free.

"I figured if you were going to stalk me, the least I could do was let you catch up." He released my arm and gave me a lopsided grin.

"I wasn't stalking you!" I gasped out.

"You're not?" He raised an eyebrow and glanced over my shoulder back toward the bike shop.

"Of course not. I didn't know you'd be at Dragons of Decatur. That was a coincidence. I waited because I just want to talk to you for a second." My entire body had heated a few degrees from my mounting embarrassment. Dealing with an ex-lover in a professional capacity was way outside my comfort zone.

"So talk," he said, glancing down at my shirt again.

I felt my cheeks burn. And even though he didn't deserve any explanation, I said, "The damn button broke, okay? I'm aware I'm flashing the goods. That everything about this—" I waved at my chest "—screams look here! But that wasn't my intention."

His brow creased as he pressed his lips into a thin line. "You probably shouldn't have gone into see Ryker like that. Now he thinks you're trying to manipulate him."

I sighed and tugged the shirt together again, feeling judged even though his tone had been neutral. "Do you really think I'd have gone in there like this if I'd known?"

"No. I guess not." He shoved his hands into his jeans pockets and glanced around. "Well, Agent Bella, now that you have me here, what is it I can do for you?"

A vision of the two of us, naked, in that hotel room we'd shared flashed in my mind.

Jesus.

I shook my head trying to dislodge the dangerous vision.

"Bella?" Wren peered at me. "Are you feeling okay?"

"I'm fine. Just a little low blood sugar. Can we go somewhere? A café or something?" I bit down on my bottom lip, an old tick I'd thought I'd kicked years ago.

"You're nervous," he said, his lips curving into a knowing smile.

"Only because while we stand here, more exposed than my chest, I can't see what's happening behind me. Can we please go somewhere so we can talk?"

Wren cast a long slow glance down my body and when he finally met my gaze, the heat I saw there, nearly made me combust. If we'd been anywhere other than the middle of the sidewalk, there was no doubt we'd already be clawing each other's clothes off.

I shook my head. "Stop. This isn't the time

or place for that."

That smile of his turned wolfish and I actually took a step back.

"So…later then?" he asked.

My stomach fluttered with anticipation, but I swallowed the agreement poised on my lips. He was part of my case. I could not continue to sleep with him. It was against protocol. "Um, can we discuss that over drinks?"

Something that looked suspiciously like triumph flashed in his eyes. "Sure, gorgeous. I know just the place." He held out his hand to me.

I stared at it, knowing if I touched him my resolve would crumble faster than a stale shortbread cookie.

"Come on, Bella," he said with a laugh. "I've touched you in a lot more intimate places."

Crap. That heat was flushing my cheeks again.

He took a step forward, grabbed my hand, and was lacing his fingers between mine before I could react.

But then everything inside me settled, and the hollowness I'd been living with the last few weeks vanished. The warmth of his hand quieted everything inside me. My thoughts were clear. And finally, *finally*, I felt in control again.

Son of a bitch.

How had I become that person? The one that needed a man to settle her nerves. Especially this one—a shifter. God, I was in trouble.

We walked two blocks before he nudged me into a small bistro in the residential section of the French Quarter.

"Hey, Bets, can we get a booth?" he asked

the hostess.

"Sure, Wren. Long time no see." She eyed our still-joined hands. "Is this your girlfriend?"

"Yes," he said and winked at me. "It's kind of a special occasion, so if we could get a little bit of privacy, that'd be great."

At his yes, pleasure wound through me and I nearly scowled at my reaction. What was wrong with me? He hadn't meant it.

"Sure." She smiled at me, but it was forced, and the warmth she'd shown while talking to Wren had vanished. This chick looked like she'd just as soon stab me as seat me in a booth with Wren. "This way."

She strode across the half-empty restaurant, tossing her hair over her shoulder and swaying her hips so hard, I thought she was going to break something.

I rolled my eyes while Wren grinned at me.

"Is this okay?" she asked him, waving to a secluded booth.

"Perfect. Can we get two waters and a bottle of your house Cabernet? We'll also need the crab cakes and the tri tip medallions. Extra bread, too."

"Sure thing." She didn't even glance at me to see if there was anything I wanted.

"Hungry?" I asked him.

"Very. What do you think? Lamb or Duck?"

"You're going to order something else?" I glanced at the menu and contemplated just getting dessert. Ever since the waiter back at the café had tried to tempt me with flourless chocolate cake, I'd had a craving.

"Have to. Occupational hazard. I can't leave here without knowing what the chef is up to."

"I see." I smiled at him, enjoying the normalcy of the conversation for just a moment.

Bets arrived with our water and wine glasses. She filled Wren's and ignored mine.

"Well, don't I feel special," I said, watching her go.

"Forget her." He passed his glass to me and poured one for himself. "Now, tell me what you were doing with Ryker."

I took a sip of my wine. "You first."

He gave me a slow smile. "You tracked me down, remember?"

Dammit.

Tapping my fingers on the table, I gave him a questioning glance. "Mr. Davenne," I said conversationally, "Are you withholding information from the FBI?"

He sat back and draped his arm across the

back of the booth. Narrowing his eyes, he said, "I wasn't aware this was an interrogation."

"No. Of course not," I said quickly, and gave him an awkward smile. So much for my subtle flirting. If one could call it that. "Sorry. It was a joke. Not a good one, obviously."

He sat there for a moment, just staring at me, and then he chuckled. "You're cute when you're flustered."

"Cute?" I frowned, all embarrassment vanishing. "I am *not* cute."

"Yes you are." Then his smile fell as he leaned in. "And I'd be happy to talk about that all day, but we have more important things to discuss."

"Things you learned from Ryker?" I asked, staring him in the eye, grateful we were getting down to business. Dealing with someone I was attracted to had never been my strong suit. Working cases and bringing down the bad guys left me much more surefooted.

"Yes." He slid an envelope over to me. "It's the only lead Ryker has."

I tilted my head as I read the invitation, instantly recognizing the business Charlie's Little Darlings. Disgust rolled through me. More than half the evidence we'd gathered on that dirt bag hadn't even been admissible in court due to questionable witnesses. Charlie was the worst humanity had to offer. I glanced up at Wren. "Looks like we have an auction to attend."

"We?" He took a small sip of wine, eyeing me.

"Yes. You and me. After I change."

His gaze traveled to my cleavage and a muscle pulsed in his clenched jaw. "Good plan."

CHAPTER 4
WREN

Bella led me into the entry of a large craftsman in the Uptown neighborhood. The old house had wood floors and an ornate wooden staircase nestled against the right wall.

"My apartment's on the top floor." She took off up the stairs, her dark hair swinging.

I followed and felt a smile tug at my lips as my gaze landed on her round ass. Goddamn, she was sexy. Curves in all the right places; deep soulful eyes; tough, kickass personality; and a fucking minx in the bedroom.

The way she'd climbed all over me, took me in her mouth, and then rode me until she'd taken her fill, had left me with my mind blown. But more than that, the way she felt in my arms afterward as she slept beside me had left me with a peace I hadn't experience before. One I wanted to experience every night.

"Jesus," I muttered and cupped the back of my neck. Now wasn't exactly the most opportune time to be contemplating peeling her clothes off and pleasuring her until she was crying my name.

Bella paused at the top of the stairs and turned back to me. "What's that?"

"You heard that, huh?"

She nodded. "Sounded like you were praying."

I let out a low chuckle and stopped one step

below her. Snaking my arm around her waist, I pulled her close and dipped my head, pausing right before our lips met.

She sucked in a sharp breath and stared at my mouth.

"Bella?"

"Yes?" she breathed.

"I've wanted you every minute since we walked out of that hotel room a few weeks ago."

Her chest rose as she took a deep breath and the shirt popped open again.

"So perfect." I trailed my fingers over the creamy flesh of her breast.

She closed her eyes and tilted her head back, giving me even more access.

Any argument for putting this moment on hold fled my mind. The electricity sparking between us was too strong. I was lost in her, unable and unwilling to stop whatever was happening between us. Pushing the shirt over her shoulder, I dipped my head once again and kissed her exposed flesh.

"Hmm," she murmured and curled her hands into my shirt. "More."

Yes. I tightened one arm around her and cupped her ass, pulling her closer, pressing my hips into her, grinding against her softness.

She moaned and her creamy skin flushed with heat as a tiny shudder ran through her. "Kiss me, Wren. Kiss me like you're a starving man."

I lifted my head and stared into her whisky-colored eyes. "Not like, am." Then I dipped my head and covered her mouth with mine, devouring her.

Our tongues warred, teased, tasted, and

everything around me faded away. All I knew was her sweet taste and her sinful body wrapped around mine… until a door slammed below.

"Bella?" an older woman called up from the bottom of the stairs. "What are you doing there with that young man?"

We froze and then Bella carefully extracted herself from my arms. A flush flooded her face as she yanked her shirt back on.

"That's coming right back off as soon as I get you inside your apartment," I whispered into her ear.

She let out a slightly choked sound and then peered over my shoulder as I twisted to follow her gaze. "Just working something out, Mrs. Prejean."

"Looks more like making out to me, dear.

Unless you want Celia's pervy boy-toy leering at y'all, you might want to wait until you're in your apartment before you start getting naked." She sent us an exaggerated wink, and then coaxed her miniature poodle out the front door.

She buried her face in her hands. "That was embarrassing."

I laughed. "Sounds like Mrs. Prejean is no stranger to a little kissing."

"Oh, God," she said and grimaced. "She can't be a day younger than eighty. I do not want to think about her with any man in any capacity."

Tugging her up the second flight of stairs, I tightened my hand around hers. "Don't worry, Bella. As soon as I get you alone, the only thing you're going to be thinking about is how good I make you feel."

Lust flashed in her eyes, but then she suddenly stiffened and blinked it away. "Wren, we have work to do. This probably isn't a good idea." But they way her voice dipped at the end, it was obvious she didn't believe her own words.

I glanced at my wristwatch and let out a relieved sigh. "We have plenty of time. Two hours."

She raised one skeptical eyebrow. "Two hours? As I recall, the last time we fell into bed together, hours went by before we came up for air."

A chuckle rumbled from my chest. "And I'd be more than happy to repeat that experience, but right now, I'll take what I can get."

The resistance melted from her expression

and her eyes lit with mischief. "I just bet you will."

Pulling her back into my arms, I stared into her sparkling eyes and said, "If I don't kiss you right now, I think I'm going to lose my mind."

"And if you do, I'm going to tear your clothes off right here in the stairwell." Her voice was hoarse, full of barely controlled passion.

"Jesus," I muttered again, and without another word, I scooped her up into my arms and took the rest of the stairs two at a time.

CHAPTER 5

BELLA

The moment we stepped into my apartment, Wren pressed me up against my closed door and buried his head against my neck, his tongue laving the sensitive area where my neck and shoulder meet.

His hands were roving, impatient as he cupped my breast with one and dug his fingers into my hip with the other. Everything heated and a shiver tingled up my spine at the same time.

No one had ever come close to eliciting the

raw, hungry response Wren was igniting inside me. It was overwhelming, yet completely empowering, and suddenly I wanted, no *needed*, to be in charge.

"Wren?" I said, gently pushing him back.

He lifted his head and dropped his hands, confusion mixing with the desire swimming in his eyes. "What is it? What's wrong?"

I smiled slowly as I undid the button of my jeans, and then stepped out of them, leaving me in nothing but my black silk lace. "Nothing's wrong."

His eyes widened, then narrowed as he reached for me, his chest muscles rippling in anticipation beneath his T-shirt.

I shook my head, enjoying the effect I was having on him. "Not yet. Strip first."

He paused for just a second, then his lips

turned up into an easy smile. "Want me to do that to music?"

"Maybe next time," I said as I slipped the strap of my bra down one arm and then the other before discarding it completely.

His gaze dropped to my chest and all humor left his expression. "Yeah. Next time." Kicking his shoes off, he reached behind his head and pulled the T-shirt off, revealing pure perfection. Wide shoulders, narrow waist, well-defined abs. Just the right amount of muscle to make every part of me quiver. Goddamn, he was gorgeous.

More gorgeous than I remembered. Or maybe it was just that I hadn't taken the time to appreciate him they way I was now.

I cleared my throat. "The jeans. Lose them."

"Gladly." A second later, he kicked his jeans

and boxer briefs to the side and stood before me, his shaft rock hard.

"Your turn," he said.

"Not yet." I reached for a throw pillow sitting in the arm chair at the edge of my living space and kneeled on it as I got to my knees before him. "This first." Wrapping my hand around the base of his cock, I smiled up at him.

"Bella, you don't—"

"Shh." I took him in my mouth, running my tongue over his tip. And when he buried his hand in my hair, I took him deeper, stroking him with each bob of my head. His breathing quickened, and his body trembled with pleasure.

An ache formed between my thighs and my breasts became heavy as my own need heightened. I wanted to experience everything with this man. Make him lose control. Feel him under me, over me, tasting me. For him to give me all of himself, as I gave myself over to him.

I quickened my pace, kissing, stroking, sucking.

"Bella," Wren breathed. "Oh, God, Bella."

Still stroking his shaft, I glanced up at him through lowered lashes and smiled. "You're glorious."

His eyes darted from where I held him and back to my face. "And you're the most beautiful thing I've ever seen."

Before I could respond, he reached down and lifted me up. My legs automatically wrapped around his waist, positioning his shaft in exactly the right spot. Pleasure shot through me as I ground into him, desperate for that delicious friction.

"I hope you aren't too attached to these," he said as his hands found my lace panties.

I opened my mouth to reassure him I wasn't, but I was too late. He'd already ripped them to shreds as he tore them off me. Then he worked his hand between us and plunged two fingers into my center.

"Ah!" I cried out, and gripped his shoulders, holding on as my muscles instantly tightened around him. I came fast and hard, taken completely by surprise.

"So fucking hot, Bella," Wren said into my ear. "I love it when you come for me."

Gasping out a breath, I said, "More."

He let out a low chuckle. "Much more, love. Much, much, more."

Without being directed, Wren carried me across the room and straight into my bedroom.

The shades were drawn, blocking out the early afternoon sun, leaving the room cool from the blasting air-conditioning. But I wasn't cold. Not even close. I was hot all over.

Wren cupped my ass and then leaned over, laying me on my back on top of my feather down comforter. "You're mine, Bella. All mine."

I nodded, more than happy to give myself over to him.

His expression changed to one of pure hunger as his pupils dilated. A small growl rose from deep in his throat as he kissed me, his lips searing mine with a passion so fierce, I felt as if he could be branding me.

And I wanted him to. Knew he was a wolf. Knew if he asked to make me his, mark me as his mate, I'd welcome his bite and be content to share his bed forever. To stand beside him for the rest of our eternity.

Under any other circumstances, I was sure that thought would've scared me senseless. But with him above me, his hands exploring my bare body, and his kiss driving out every other thought, I was his for the taking.

He broke away and stood up, with me still lying at the end of the bed.

A chill dampened the fire that had been raging in me, but it vanished the moment he placed his palm on my chest with just the slightest amount of pressure, and ran it down the center of my body. Slowly he spread my legs and once again wrapped them around his waist. A small shudder of anticipation shook me as I lay there, my eyes locked on his intense gaze.

I had the feeling he had a window straight

into my soul. The fire, the cravings, my deep-seated need to be wanted. To belong to and be one with another. To finally walk the earth with someone who claimed me as his.

Wren shifted his hips, and slid his erection along my slick folds, not yet entering me.

My breath hitched as I closed my eyes, reveling in the feel of him.

"The ecstasy on your face is intoxicating," he said, and gripped my hips hard as he entered me in one smooth thrust.

"Ahh," I moaned with his intrusion. "Yes."

He held me tight to him and slowly circled his hips, the movement incredibly erotic.

"Wren," I breathed.

"Tell me what you want, Bella." His sensual command was full of wicked promise.

"Make love to me."

He shook his head. "No. Tell me what you specifically want. Slow and torturous or hard and rough. How do you want me to make you mine?"

Make you mine. The words echoed in my mind as everything in me longed to respond, *bite me. Make me your mate.*

But that was the last thing I could say. Not here. Not now. We barely knew each other. His words were for sexual gratification only. And even though, deep down, I knew I wanted so much more, the physical relationship was enough… for now.

"Hard," I gasped out, unable to hold back any longer. "Fast and hard until I'm delirious with sensation."

Determination flashed through his eyes as his fingers dug into my hips. "Touch yourself."

My eyes widened as I stared at him.

"I want to watch you pleasure yourself while I fuck you."

A bolt of electric heat shot straight to my center. I gasped and moved my hand to my most sensitive spot, obeying his command.

And then he started to move. Keeping my hips still with his vice-like grip, he deliberately thrust into me, slow at first, taking his time to savor our joining.

I lowered my gaze, watching his cock slide in and out of me, my desire consuming me as I worked over the exquisite bundle of nerves with my fingers.

"That's it, Bella. Show me how you like it."

I bit down hard on my bottom lip and kept my gaze on his erection as he made love to me, completely lost to sensation.

And then suddenly he quickened his pace, slamming into me hard, over and over again hitting just the right spot.

The pressure built, my muscles clenching around him, and a high-pitched cry ripped from my lips as I grabbed for his waist and froze. The orgasm crashed through me, taking my breath away, and when I finally came down, I met Wren's glittering wild eyes and smiled. "That was… perfect."

"You're perfect," he said, and leaned down helping himself to my breast. His teeth scraped lightly over my nipple, eliciting a shiver of pleasure.

"Oh, God. How do you do that?" I asked as I wrapped my legs tighter around his waist, already primed for more.

A ghost of a smile claimed his lips as he

cupped my breast with one hand, and used his thumb and forefinger to squeeze my nipple while he pumped his hips. I closed my eyes and lost myself in him, welcoming every pinch and bite that sent pleasure-filled pain straight to my center.

"Yes," I said when he bit down on my nipple, and I gripped his ass, urging him deeper. He filled me completely, taking everything I had to offer. And when his breathing finally became ragged and his body jerked above me, I reached between us and pressed down on my clit once more, making us both cry in unison as we toppled over the edge into mind-numbing ecstasy.

Afterward, we lay side by side on my bed with Wren lazily tracing circles on my abdomen. I stretched, feeling like the feline who'd been utterly and completely satisfied.

"We'll be doing that again," Wren said in a matter-of-fact tone.

I turned and raised an eyebrow. "Today?"

"If I have any say about it."

I glanced at the wall clock. "I don't think there's time before our appointment."

"I know. But I wanted to make myself perfectly clear." He turned on his side and pierced me with his intense gaze. "This isn't a fling anymore. Not for me. And I plan to spend a lot more time right here in this bed. You game?"

I narrowed my eyes at him. "Just my bed?"

He shook his head. "No. Dinner. Movies. Music. Whatever you want. Just know I'm going to discover every single sinful way to make your body shudder like that, and I'm going to know exactly how every inch of your body tastes."

"That sounds… indulgent," I said, my mouth suddenly dry.

"Damn straight it is. Any objections?"

A ball of warmth materialized right in the middle of my chest. He wanted me just as much as I wanted him. I reached up and pressed my palm to his cheek and then gave him a slow seductive kiss. When I broke away, I said, "No objections."

CHAPTER 6
WREN

I T WAS A damn good thing Bella had changed into jeans and a T-shirt that covered all her assets, because the doorman at the warehouse was the worst kind of sleaze. Instead of looking her in the eye, he swept his gaze along her body and kept it glued to her ass as he waved us in. My wolf rose up, ready to strike, but I pushed the urge down as I grabbed her hand possessively. Now wasn't the time.

He was so distracted he didn't even take time to check if we were on the guest list.

Though our fake ID names would've been there. Ryker had seen to that. After lunch, I'd sent him a message we were going to check it out and he'd had his contact send an RSVP.

"Well, well, well, what do we have here? You two looking for something to spice up the bedroom?" A short, balding man in a shiny, gray suit smiled, showing his coffee-stained teeth. "I have everything you could possibly imagine. Barely legals, girl on girl, threesomes, foursomes, male on male." He pumped his eyebrows, looking utterly ridiculous as he tried to sell us his smut prints. "Pretty much anything but bestiality. That's next week's show."

Bella's hand tightened around mine, and her body tensed as if she was already prepared to fight.

"I think we'll just take a look around," I said

to the salesman. "We'll let you know if we need any help."

"Sure. Sure." He waved a hand. "Just remember, no pictures allowed, except by us of course." Nodding toward the surveillance camera in the corner, he grinned. "Anything that happens here is fair game. Consider yourselves warned."

After he walked back to his makeshift desk behind a white folding table, Bella leaned in and whispered, "What did he mean by that? Fair game?"

I turned her slightly to the left so the one other couple in the building was in her sightline. They were middle-aged, slightly overweight, and completely oblivious to their surroundings. The man had his woman pressed up against the rough wall, and his hand was shoved between her legs as she sucked on his neck. Beside them was a photo of a gorgeous, curvy blonde masturbating while a man in the shadows watched.

"Whoa." Bella turned her head sharply back toward me. "Is this a makeshift sex club?"

I shrugged. "No idea. But looks like it might be standard operating procedure for this place. So let's just take a look around and get out of here. Quickly. And keep your back turned to the camera. We don't need footage of either one of us in this place floating around out there."

Her jaw flexed as she ground her teeth. "No. Even though this will go in the official report, if a tape leaks, this sort of thing won't help either of us."

"Let's take a look around before we interrogate the creepster running this thing," I said and guided her away from the live sex show going on right in front of us.

She nodded. We had to look interested; otherwise our questions would be too suspicious, and no doubt, we'd be shut down fast.

"Most of these aren't as bad as I'd imagined they would be," Bella said, eyeing an artsy black and white photo of two women kissing.

"Huh." I rubbed my jaw. She was right. I'd expected images closer to those on a hardcore porn sight. "Makes you wonder why they went to the trouble of making it so exclusive."

"Maybe to make it seem more special? To charge more?" She moved on to another black and white that showed a man lying on top of a woman, scraping his teeth over her nipple. There was nothing sleazy about it. It was one hundred percent sensual.

"Maybe." I averted my gaze, still uncomfortable. No matter what it looked like on the surface, this was still put on by Charlie's people. There was no way I believed they were toning down their operation.

We walked past a temporary partition, and Bella let out a tiny gasp. The clean white walls had been splattered with red paint, made to look like blood running from the ceiling. Jagged, demeaning words such as whore, bitch, and slut were carved at random below each of the haunting photographs.

And as awful as the effects were, the setting was nothing compared to the subjects of the photos. They were also in black and white, but nothing about them said sensual.

Isolated. Demeaned. Tortured.

Those were the words that came to mind as I stared in horror at the naked, whip-marked woman enclosed in a cage barely large enough for her slight frame. Her eyes were squeezed tightly shut, and her arms wrapped around her body as if she was trying to will herself into any other reality. And if that wasn't bad enough, off to the right was a shadow of a man lounging in a chair, one leg stretched out and a whiskey glass in his hand as he sat there, watching.

But the image to the left is what really put me over the edge. It was a sign that read *Augustine's*. Horror, combined with uncontrollable rage, rose up from the depths of my soul.

I knew without a shadow of a doubt that nothing about the photo was staged. Augustine's was an alligator meat processing warehouse where the traffickers had been holding my brother's mate before they had a chance to sell her off.

"Oh my God," Bella said in a hushed whisper beside me.

"Do you recognize it, too?" I asked, still staring at the photo.

"It?" She pointed. "Don't you mean him?"

I cut my gaze to the photo she was pointing at. "Holy fuck."

"He's guilty," she said.

There was no doubt about it. The photo she pointed at was of the same woman. In this shot she was sitting on a cement floor, hugging her knees, with her head twisted as she glared at the man standing just a few feet from her—the man who was supposed to protect her: FBI Agent Fischer.

CHAPTER 7

BELLA

My stomach rolled, and my mouth watered as if I was going to be sick. The truth was staring back at me in that print. There was no more denying it. My fellow FBI agent was part of the trafficking ring.

He was the mole.

The reason Bax Carter had died. He'd been Fischer's partner, and now there was no doubt in my mind, Carter had found something on Fischer. The only question that remained was if Fischer had killed Bax himself or if he'd hired a hitman.

I straightened my spine and waved the slimy curator over.

"Have you found something you like?"

I wanted to smack his shit-eating grin right off his face. But ever the professional, I relaxed my shoulders and gave him a sultry smile. "Yes. Him." I pointed to the photo. "I was wondering if you could put us in touch with him."

His eyes clouded and he peered at us suspiciously. "Why?"

Wren frowned and opened his mouth to speak, but I wrapped my arm around his and leaned in close as I cut him off. "My boyfriend and I, well, how do I put this?" I smiled sheepishly at Wren, who narrowed his eyes at me. "We kind of like it when someone's, ah…watching, if you get my drift."

The curator's lips curved into a knowing grin as he nodded in Wren's direction. "Got yourself a naughty one, don't you?"

Wren's expression darkened, but he said nothing.

The other man laughed heartily. "What I wouldn't do to film the two of you."

Wren's muscles twitched beneath my grip and I tightened my hold, willing him to not tear the man's head off.

"That's flattering," I said sweetly. "But neither of us wants that much attention. Is it possible to get in touch with this man? He has the right…look."

The curator cast an appraising glance down my body. "Possibly. But it's going to cost you."

I shrugged. "I expected nothing less."

"Not money," he said, as an evil glint

flashed in his greedy eyes. "Photos."

"Excuse me?" Wren said, his tone low and barely controlled.

The curator waved a hand at the prints. "This is where we're putting our resources right now. Erotic art. If you want Shade, you'll have to let our photographer in, too."

"Fine," I said. "When?"

He handed me a card. "Shade will be in touch."

"Soon?"

"That depends," Mr. Slime said.

"On?" My skin was starting to crawl at the hungry look on his face.

"How much you spend here today. Customers who show their appreciation are given first priority in this business. And you're in luck, because even though this is an auction, we have buy-it-nows for all our items."

"Of course you do," Wren said dryly. "Since my girlfriend is so enchanted with…Shade? Is that what you called him?"

Mr. Slime nodded.

"Then we'll take that one." He pointed to the print.

"And this one," I said, feeling the bile rise up in the back of my throat.

Wren turned and caught sight of the print I was looking at. It featured his brother's mate, Thea. She was standing in a cell, topless, wearing only a short skirt and a broken expression as she stared at the camera. Remnants of a cotton shirt were strewn on the floor in front of her as if it had been ripped off.

Wren snarled, and suddenly he lunged forward, his body contorting and his bones cracking as he shifted into a magnificent black wolf.

The curator let out a high-pitched shriek and stumbled backward, but he was no match for the angry wolf who plowed him down and grabbed him by the throat with powerful jaws.

"Wren!" I cried, running forward, my hand already reaching for the gun tucked against the small of my back.

Wren growled, holding the man in place.

"Jesus," I whispered, taking in the scene. Our cover was completely blown. I had two choices: call in the Feds and hand over the picture of Thea, who'd testify to being held captive, or search the place myself first. I made a snap decision and hurried back into the front part of the warehouse. The couple that had been making out against the wall had vanished.

I let out a small sigh of relief. At least we were alone. I jogged to the front door, noted the doorman was wandering the parking area, a phone pressed to his ear and a cigarette dangling out of his mouth. Hopefully he'd stay busy. I turned the deadbolt, and hurried back to Wren and the curator. They were in the same position as when I'd left them.

"I don't know what you plan to do with him now, but I'm going to search his desk for any information."

"Who are you?" the curator wailed.

"None of your concern," I said in my steely FBI voice as I yanked the top drawer of his desk open. A smart phone lay on top of a stack of papers. I pulled it out and pressed the on button. Damn. It was passcode protected. "What's the passcode to this?"

"None of your fucking business, bitch," Slimy said. He swung his fist wildly into the side of Wren's head, knocking the wolf off of him. Slimy scrambled back, kicking out at Wren. But Wren, already back on his feet, dodged him easily and locked his jaws onto the man's biceps.

"No!" Slimy cried, trying to wrench his arm from Wren. The wolf only tightened his hold and shook his head, shaking his victim violently, until Slimy stilled.

"Passcode?" I calmly asked again.

"6969," he said, weakly.

"Of course it is." I rolled my eyes and punched in the numbers. A list of contacts came up. Shade had been his last phone call. I pressed my finger to the number and waited while the phone rang.

"What?" the man on the other end snapped.

"Your business associate down at the warehouse is currently being detained by a two hundred pound wolf. I don't know what he plans to do with him, and honestly, I don't care. But you should know we have photographic proof of you engaging in the detainment of recently-abducted girls. I think you'd better start talking, or every single FBI agent in the state is going to be on your ass. I'd give it about a half hour."

"Bella?" he asked casually, seemingly unconcerned with my threat.

"Yes."

"I wondered if they'd send you." The words were light and I could hear the smile in his tone.

"You don't seem too worried." I frowned.

This was not how the call was supposed to go.

"No. I'm relieved, actually. Listen, I don't give a fuck what happens to Benny. He's first class sleaze. Right now I need your help. I've got a lead on the kingpin in charge of this trafficking ring. I'm supposed to be making an exchange, but I'm going to need backup. Can you meet me in a half hour?"

I pulled the phone away from my ear and stared at it. Then I cleared my throat. "Are you fucking kidding me?"

"No. Come on, Bella. You know how this goes. I had to play my part. Deep undercover. There was no other way."

"You're off the reservation," I said, stubbornly. Orders had come down that an agent had gone rogue. That only happened when a superior officer pulled the plug on a mission and the agent didn't comply.

"For good reason, too. I can't—dammit. Just meet me at the abandoned docks behind Federal City in forty minutes."

The line went dead before I could respond.

"Dammit!" I stared at Wren, meeting his wide wolf eyes. "We need to go."

He swiveled his head back to his captive and then back to me as if to ask, "What about him?"

I sighed and pulled my own phone out of my pocket. A second later, I said, "We have a package for you. Can you send someone to the Warehouse to pick him up?"

"Well, hello, Bella," Ryker said. "Does this mean you have some cleanup for my crew to do?"

"Yes. Wren shifted. We can't leave the little

bastard here. Besides, he might know something useful."

"I'll send a crew now, but Bella?"

"Yes?"

"This is going to cost you."

There was never any doubt. "Fine. Just do what it takes. We have an appointment to keep."

CHAPTER 8
WREN

Jesus. What had I been thinking? I hadn't. That was the problem. I'd lost control and shifted. Almost ripped that bastard's throat out before I'd been able to stop myself.

The moment I'd seen the print of Thea, exposed to her captors, I'd lost it. She was my brother's mate. Part of the pack. One of our own. Instincts kicked in and that was the end of it.

I watched Bella as I slid my jeans back on. Luckily they hadn't been torn in the shift, but my shirt had. It was a goner.

Bella was careful to keep her gaze adverted, though my bare skin wasn't anything she hadn't seen before. Touched before. Hell, kissed, clawed, and teased only an hour before. The echo of her soft lips on my chest filtered through my mind, and I instantly felt like the biggest bastard in the world.

Here we were, surrounded by prints of women who'd been held against their will, and I was selfishly thinking about the last time I'd had Bella in her bed.

I scowled just as Bella finally lifted her gaze.

"What?" She turned swiftly, checking to see if anyone had joined us.

"Nothing. I assume that was Fischer on the phone?"

"Yeah." She glanced at her watch. "We have

fifteen minutes."

There was banging on the door, followed shortly by a text on my phone. "It's Ryker's men," I told Bella as I went to let them in.

"Good. Let's go."

WE SAT IN Bella's small, white SUV on Patterson Street a block and a half away from our designated meeting place. To the right was Federal City, the now defunct Navel base and to the left was the Mississippi River. I peered through a set of binoculars at the deserted structure on the floating pier. "This isn't a great idea."

"You're right," she said, resignation in her tone. "But Fischer said he'd be here. What else are we supposed to do? Ignore that?"

"No. At least let me text Smoke and Scarlett. If they're still in town, they could be here in minutes." Smoke was a hacker for the FBI, and Scarlett was his mate, as well as Bax Carter's former girlfriend. They also happened to be part of my pack. If I trusted anyone, it was them.

"Fine, but I doubt they're going to get here in time." She pointed toward the end of the road.

A silver truck turned onto the short gravel drive that led to the pier.

"That's him," she said, making no move to climb out of her car.

I sent Smoke a text.

He replied instantly. *Be there in ten minutes. Don't lose him.*

"They're on their way." I showed the phone to Bella.

She nodded, and we both sat there, waiting. For what, exactly, I wasn't sure. But since there was a strong possibility we'd be walking into a trap, the best we could do was to wait and see.

My wolf stirred, fighting the desire to shift, to hunt, to scent out the one man who'd been wreaking havoc in our lives for the last few months. The one who was supposed to be the good guy. The one someone called when they needed help. The revulsion at his betrayal of everything he was supposed to stand for consumed me, making me nearly vibrate with it.

"You need to calm down." Bella placed her small hand on my arm. "I can feel the frustration rolling off you."

I turned to her, one eyebrow raised as I

stared at her bouncing knee. "I could say the same about you."

She stilled her leg, but instantly started a tap, tap, tap with her fingers on the steering wheel.

I shifted my gaze to her hand.

"Shit," she muttered, and clasped her hands in her lap.

Chuckling, I lifted the binoculars to peer once again at the abandoned structure. And that's when I heard it.

Rapid gunfire.

"No!" Bella bolted out of the car, her gun in her hand.

"Shit!" I scrambled, following her lead and sprinting after her. Damn she was fast. She was at the top of the gravel driveway before I finally caught her.

"Go that way." She pointed to a metal storage structure off to the right while she ran to the left, heading for the far end of the dock.

But my wolf protested. The instinct to stay with my mate was too strong. *Mate?* Where had that come from? It must've been because of our earlier activities in the bedroom. I shook my head violently, trying and failing to dislodge the instinct.

"Wren!" Bella admonished in a harsh whisper. "What are you doing?"

"Covering you."

"But—"

"Forget it. I'm not leaving your side just yet. Now go." I waved at the dock just as more gunfire sounded from the building on the floating dock.

She nodded once and then leaped from the

shore onto the dock and crouched underneath a window, her back to the wall. I followed her, amazed at her agility. It wasn't exactly a small leap. Her FBI training must've been intense.

A woman's high-pitched scream suddenly pierced the air. Bella and I exchanged a determined look, then she sprang up and peered through the window while I took off toward the slightly opened door.

Behind me, a bullet shattered through the window, and when I glanced back, I saw Bella disappearing around the back of the building. Losing sight of her hit me hard, and my wolf exploded. With a low growl, I gave myself over to the shift, welcoming the second twisting and breaking of bones. I landed on all four paws, my momentum already propelling me forward. Skidding to a stop, I used my nose to nudge the door open.

The loud creak of the rusty door was like nails on a chalkboard to my ears, and I ducked, expecting more bullets to come sailing in my direction. Instead, heated voices filled the crowded warehouse.

I scrambled behind a large crate and twitched my nose at the pungent odors of mold and grease in the air.

"Drop the gun, Fischer," a man with a gravelly voice ordered from the far side of the warehouse. He was large and imposing in an authoritative way. "The game's over. You've lost. It's time to give up."

I saw Bella shift to stand behind the large man, her gun pointed to the left-hand corner of the warehouse, straight at a tall dark-haired man who wore fatigues and had a rifle in his hands.

Fischer took a step forward, a lone ray of light illuminating him. His face was haggard, and his knuckles were white from gripping his weapon. "I'm not playing any games, *Director*."

The cold hatred in his tone was enough to stop me in my tracks. Director? Of the FBI? What was he doing here? Wasn't Bella sent to investigate? Why would he be here by himself in a showdown with Fischer? It made no sense. And why had Fischer asked us to come here?

"You know what I want. Make the exchange and I'll be gone, out of your way forever." Fischer threw a burlap sack onto the concrete floor.

"There is no way I'm giving up the girl." The director cast a quick glance at Bella, then to his right at something I couldn't see. "You've ruined enough lives with this charade you've been playing. Drop the gun and maybe you can avoid the death penalty."

Fischer's mouth dropped open in shock, then a realization seemed to come over him as he narrowed his eyes and aimed his rifle at his superior. "We're done with this negotiation."

The director dove behind a stack of crates and ordered, "Shoot him, Stone."

Bella didn't hesitate. She fired off three shots as Fischer darted straight toward me. The first two sailed past him, but the third one hit its mark, sending Fischer flying back about six feet. He crashed into a wall and fell in a heap on the floor.

"Grab the girl. He assaulted her and she's in desperate need of medical attention," the director said to Bella as he darted forward and retrieved the sack. "There's no time to wait for first responders."

I shrank back into the shadows, unwilling to expose my wolf self to the director if I didn't need to. Bella wouldn't want him to know she'd teamed up with a civilian anyway. No, I'd stay behind and make sure Fischer really was out of commission.

Bella leaned down and lifted an unconscious young woman into her arms. The woman's head lolled to the side, her long blond hair almost sweeping the floor.

"Let's go. We're running out of time," the director said, waving at Bella. "I'll send a cleanup crew for that traitor."

"You got it, boss," Bella said. As she passed me, she peered into the shadows, meeting my gaze and jerked her head, indicating I should check on Fischer. I nodded once and then retreated out of the director's view.

When they were both gone, I trotted over to the limp man, expecting the scent of his coppery blood to sting my nose. But when I inhaled, all I got was the stale smell of mold and the muddy stench of the Mississippi river.

I crept forward, keeping my head down, and nosed his shoulder.

He moaned and curled in on himself. Then his eyes popped opened and he sat straight up, clutching his head as he grimaced in pain. "Son of a bitch. Fucking bastard." Lurching forward, he tried to scramble to his feet, but he clutched his side and slid back down against the wall, breathing heavily. He glanced around, panic in his expression, before he slumped against the wall and glared at me. "He took her, didn't he?"

I snarled and paced in front of him. Was he talking about the blonde or Bella?

His expression turned murderous. "Fuck. Thanks for nothing. I told Bella to hurry because I needed backup, not so you two could help the bastard. But if you think you're taking me out of here alive, you're mistaken."

Leaning to the side, he groaned as he reached out to snag the fallen rifle, but I lunged and grabbed it with my teeth before he could get to it.

He laughed humorlessly. "I can't wait to see you try to use that thing in wolf form."

I trotted a good twenty or thirty feet away, dropped the rifle, and shifted. Standing naked in my human form once more, I lifted the rifle and aimed for his chest. "I wouldn't make any sudden movements if I were you."

"Where's Carly?"

"Who?"

"My sister. He's been holding her captive for over a week, you fuckbag."

I glanced back at the place where I'd seen Bella holding the unconscious woman. "The blonde is your sister?" I asked incredulously.

"Yes." He let out a long frustrated sigh. "Where did they go?"

Hell if I knew. "He said they were taking her to the hospital."

Fischer snapped his head up. "There's no fucking way he's taking her there. Besides, she's only drugged. Unless he gave her an overdose, she'll wake on her own."

"Drugged?" I asked, and then added, "What do you mean he's been holding her captive?"

"Exactly what I said. A few days after I went

undercover on this case, I hit the mother lode, and found a clue that led me straight to the director. Only the evidence wasn't solid enough. It was enough to make me sure he's the dirtbag in question, but not enough to convict. And because I know he killed my partner Bax, I wasn't letting him walk."

There was no faking the hatred in his tone. And the pure disgust rolling off him was enough to make me lower the rifle to my side.

He watched the movement, and with a nod of acknowledgement, he continued. "When he realized I was after him, he started planting evidence to implicate me. Flimsy, circumstantial evidence, but enough to make the FBI start getting suspicious. But I wasn't backing down, you know? They killed Bax, then went after Scarlett because they thought she had information, though they gave up on her when they realized she didn't."

The wind blew through the warehouse, rattling the metal sides. I ignored it and asked, "Where does your sister come in?"

A shadow fell over his face. "After one of his fixers almost took out Scarlett, I requested a leave of absence. I didn't know who I could or couldn't trust. So I went deep undercover on my own. I knew all along it was risky, that I could be made at any time, but I didn't feel I had a choice."

I nodded, encouraging him.

"Then one night when I was on a run to meet with a potential buyer, I was recognized. The director got wind I was still after him and kidnapped my sister. That was right after your pack mate Thea was rescued. Everything I've done since then has been to get my sister back. I was supposed to buy her from that sleazebag and leave the country. I was going to take him down today, but then Bella took his word over mine and here we are."

My gaze landed on where the burlap sack had been. "How much did you give him?"

"Every cent I had, brother. Every goddamned cent my parents ever left us both."

"Fuck." I ran a hand through my hair, unsure what to do.

"Dude. I know you're a wolf, but can you cover yourself, please? You're making me uncomfortable."

Right. I'd forgotten. Keeping a grip on the rifle, I hurried out the door and grabbed my clothes that had been shoved behind an old oil barrel. No doubt that had been Bella's handiwork. She wouldn't have wanted the director to see my jeans strewn over the dock. Then I returned to find Fischer struggling to get to his feet.

It was then I noticed there wasn't a speck of blood anywhere. Bella had shot him, hadn't she? "Why aren't you bleeding?"

Using the hand he had resting on his abdomen, he lifted his shirt, revealing a Kevlar vest. "You don't think I'd come to a gun fight with just a knife do you?"

Of course he wouldn't. He was FBI as well. Rogue, but still FBI. I held out a hand to him.

He stared at it for a moment, then grabbed hold as I helped him up. "We have to get out of here. He'll be sending a cleanup crew."

Just as the words were out of his mouth, the rumble of a truck sounded outside.

"Shit." He glanced around, panic in his expression.

I peered out the door and felt the tension drain from my shoulders. "Relax. It's Smoke and Scarlett."

He pressed himself to the wall. "You better go out first. If they see me, they might shoot first and ask questions later."

I doubted it. They were both from neighborhoods that dealt in all shades of gray. If anyone was going to listen to him, it was them. But even though I was giving him the benefit of the doubt regarding his story, he appeared to be hovering on the edge of a breakdown. It was better if I explained.

Stepping outside, I waved them over.

"Where's Bella?" Scarlett asked.

A ball of unease rolled through my gut. Was

she all right? If Fischer was telling the truth, she was in grave danger, even if she didn't know it yet. "I'll explain everything later, but right now we need to get out of here."

Smoke nodded and they both jogged back to the truck.

"I have Fischer."

Smoke froze. "Shade is here?"

Scarlett turned wide eyes on me. "You trust him?"

"I have to." I poked my head into the warehouse. "Let's go."

Fischer hobbled behind me as we made our way to Smoke's truck. And just after we both climbed into the back seat, a line of three black SUVs came tearing down Patterson toward us. "Go!" I ordered. "It's the cleanup crew. They've come for Fischer."

Smoke didn't hesitate. He put the truck in gear and took off. But as the truck jerked forward, there was no missing Smoke's penetrating stare at Fischer in the rearview mirror. "If I find out you're on the wrong side of this, I'll end you myself. Got it?"

Fischer didn't flinch as he met his colleague's intense stare. After a moment, he nodded once. "If I am, I'll pull the trigger myself."

CHAPTER 9

BELLA

I SAT IN the back of Director Ralston's Cadillac Escalade with the unconscious girl's head in my lap. She was breathing, but she hadn't moved or woken once. "Hurry. I think she needs a doctor sooner rather than later."

"There's one waiting." He glanced over his shoulder, his round face red with heavy circles under his pale blue eyes. "Hand me your cell phone."

I fished it out of my pocket and passed it to him, making a mental note I needed to get in touch with Wren as soon as possible. There was no need to worry about him. He could take care of himself, but I didn't want him worrying about me.

Ralston palmed the phone, scrolled through my last phone calls, and then swore under his breath. "Why were you dealing with the dragons?"

My head snapped up. "Information. I was just doing my job, sir. It's what led me to The Warehouse and then the docks."

He muttered something unintelligible, lowered the window, and threw my phone onto the freeway. I watched as the car behind us, rolled right over it.

"Why the hell did you do that?" I scowled at him.

"Everything is traceable."

"Who would be following us? I shot Fischer." My blood pressure spiked and my body heated. While this scenario had at first seemed unusual, it was now so far out of the norm, I was starting to feel claustrophobic.

Then I heard it.

Click.

The sound of the automatic locks sliding into place.

"Ralston? What exactly is going on?" I asked through clenched teeth, as I automatically reached for my firearm and blanched with horror when I realized it wasn't in my holster where I'd left it. "Where is my 9 mm?"

"I'm sorry, Stone. When we put you on the case, you were so new to the field we never thought you'd get this close. It's unfortunate that you've been caught up in this, but now that you are, there's really no other choice."

A hole the size of Texas materialized in my chest. The director had been a mentor of mine when I'd joined the FBI. He was the one person I'd trusted above all others. And when he'd said to shoot Fischer, there'd been no reason for me to disobey his command.

Only now it was clear to me Fischer had been telling the truth the entire time, and my surrogate father had not only betrayed me, but his country, too.

It didn't escape my notice that he hadn't answered my question about my firearm. No doubt he'd lifted it while we'd been getting Carly into the car. My heart lodged in my throat and I had to swallow hard. "No other choice than what?"

"I really am sorry, but it's better than the alternative." He slowed, shifted into the right lane, and took the freeway exit.

His matter-of-fact, monotone answer and the way he kept his gaze straight ahead as if he'd made his final decision sent a chill up my spine. I clutched the unconscious woman and felt completely helpless. We were trapped in a luxury SUV with arguably the most powerful and most dangerous man in the department.

I eyed the seats, looking for something, anything. A weapon of any sort. Then I scoped out the back cargo area. Nothing. Not even an emergency roadside toolkit.

"When we get to the cargo ship, things will go much smoother for you if you just do as I say."

"Cargo ship?" I forced the words out between my dry lips, feeling as if all the fight had been beaten out of me.

"How else are you going to get to Russia?"

"Russia?" He was selling me to the sex trade. He was the one who'd killed Bax Carter. He really was at the center of everything.

"Yes. They pay very well. I've been assured our girls are treated with high regard—as long as they keep quiet and do as they are told." His cold, dead stare reflected back at me in the rearview mirror. "You might have some trouble."

At his words, rage rose from the depths of my soul, overtaking me and I flew off my seat, reaching for him.

He ducked and swerved, nearly taking out a small Toyota in the next lane. "Sit the fuck down, Storm. Are you trying to get us killed?"

The car swerved again to the right, sending

me crashing into the passenger's side. "No. Only you," I spat.

Before I could recover, he reached down and produced a handgun. Using his left hand, he pointed it right at me. "Try that again, and I'll shoot you dead. Got it, agent?"

I glared at him, almost preferring he shoot me. The memory of firing at Fischer flashed in my mind and made my stomach roll. Holy God. I'd shot him, and he'd been the good guy. I closed my eyes and prayed I hadn't killed him, and that he was working with Wren at that very moment to find us.

"That's better. Now, see if you can wake Carly. We're almost there. She's more valuable if she's conscious."

"More valuable?" I echoed, horrified I'd ever looked up to the evil man sitting less than two feet from me.

"Don't be so naïve, Storm. This is the price we pay for diplomatic cooperation. We do favors for them, and they do favors for us. It's how the world works."

"Not mine."

He ignored me and sped up, as a man dressed all in black and holding a rifle waved us through a gate, onto a gravel road that was lined with cypress trees.

I glanced down at Carly and smoothed her hair back. Her breathing was stronger than it had been before. As I watched her, I soothed as best I could. "Everything's going to be okay. You don't have to worry. We'll get out of this somehow."

Ralston snorted his amusement from the front seat.

"And by the time this day is over, I promise the man responsible for doing this to you is going to be dead."

Her eyes flew open and she pierced me with a stare so focused, I wondered how long she'd actually been awake. "Make him suffer." She forced the words out in a voice so raspy, I could barely understand her.

"Count on it," I whispered.

The Cadillac jerked to a stop in front of an old, rotted, wooden dock. A large rust-orange cargo ship loomed above. Ralston kept his gun trained on me the entire time he exited the car.

Carly sat up, and for the first time I noted the bruises covering one of her shoulders and both wrists.

"What did they do to you?" I asked, unable to disguise the horror in my tone.

"They tied me to a radiator and left me there for days."

"They? Ralston and someone else?"

She nodded, tears filling her big brown eyes. "The other one is a mean bastard."

As the tears rolled down her cheeks, my resolve to make Ralston pay solidified. I raised my gaze, spotted Ralston talking to a tall thin man with shaggy, dirty-blond hair. There was something eerily familiar about him that made my skin crawl.

"That's him." Carly's voice shook as she shuddered.

"Do you know his name?" I asked, as the man turned and locked eyes with me. His thin lips curved up into a sinister smile that had long ago been burned into my memory.

Recognition sucker-punched me in the gut,

rendering me speechless for a moment.

"Ralston calls him—"

"Jay Auden."

She let out a little gasp. "You know him?"

My entire body was numb as I turned and stared her dead in the eye. "He had a twin. I killed him five days before I turned eighteen years old."

CHAPTER 10
WREN

"Dammit!" I shoved my phone in my pocket after Bella's phone went straight to voicemail for the fifth time in a row.

"She's not going to answer," Fischer said as we sped down the bayou road toward the resort my family owned. "If she's part of his team, it's too risky. And if she isn't, he's already discarded it."

"Bella isn't involved in anything that bastard has going on," I said with a distinct growl in my tone.

He shrugged. "Whatever you say, man. But you should know she has a connection to his partner."

"What the hell are you talking about?" My wolf was coiled tightly, ready to strike if Fischer made one wrong move.

Fischer held my gaze, his shoulders stiff and expression dead serious. "She dated his brother a long time ago. His twin brother."

"Jay Auden is his partner?" Smoke said from the driver's seat.

Fischer nodded and went back to staring out the window.

"You knew all this?" I peered at Smoke, a scowl claiming my lips.

"Sorry, man. After Thea was attacked and Bella showed up, I did my homework on her." He shifted his gaze to Fischer. "This entire case is a clusterfuck and trust is hard to come by."

"Jesus." I grabbed the edge of the seat and clamped my mouth shut.

"There's more, but maybe we should wait until we get to the resort." Smoke cast a glance at Scarlett who was busy tapping away on a smart phone. "Got anything yet?"

"I'm not sure." She bit her bottom lip and squinted as she stared at the screen. "What exactly am I looking for?"

"Anyone who lists South Louisiana as their location." Smoke glanced back at me and Fischer. "I have her searching any possible informants or unofficial assets to see if we can get a lead on Ralston."

Fischer closed his eyes. "I've been trolling that site for days. There's nothing."

Scarlett let out an impatient sigh, then she

sat straight up. "What about this one? Double J, South Louisiana, ties to the shipping industry."

Fischer twisted. "Let me see that."

Scarlett held the phone out to him to take a look but didn't hand it over. It was Smoke's phone and it was full of bells and whistles for tracking people down and hacking just about anything with capacity to get online.

Fischer eyed the phone. "Son of a bitch. That message wasn't there two days ago." He whipped out his own phone and tapped a message. One came back instantly. He grinned a dark twisted smile of satisfaction. "Got him."

"How?" Smoke and I asked at the same time.

"An informant of mine. Make the next left. We've got a location."

Smoke stared at him from the rearview mirror and then narrowed his eyes as he pulled over. "That was entirely too easy, Shade. I'm going to need more than an informant."

"Fuck!" Fischer slammed his fist down on the back of the driver's seat. "He has my sister. And this one's fuck buddy." He jabbed his thumb in my direction. "We don't have time for this bullshit."

"What we don't have time for, is being played," Smoke said, while I struggled to not deck Fischer for talking about Bella that way. "Tell me where we're going, who gave you the information, and why you think it's better than calling the contact number and running a trace."

"Jesus." He reached into his jeans pocket and pulled out a shiny black business card with the name *C Black* scrawled across the front with a phone number listed below. Nothing else.

Smoke glanced at it and shrugged. "So?"

"That site?" Fischer gestured to Smoke's phone. "C runs it. And we... well, we have history."

"You have a thing with Crissy?" Smoke asked, surprise coloring his tone.

"Not exactly. More like..." He shrugged. "We go back a long time."

"So far back she's willing to give you information on her clients with just a text?" Scarlett raised a skeptical eyebrow.

"Yes." The word was definitive, leaving no room for further explanation.

Smoke sent a text of his own while we all waited in silence. And when the ding sounded indicating a return text, Smoke let out a small chuckle and shook his head in mild surprise.

"Looks like Fischer's telling the truth."

Fischer gritted his teeth. "Can you start the fucking truck now?"

Smoke gave him a mock solute, fired up the truck, and peeled out, spraying gravel all over the bayou road.

CHAPTER 11

BELLA

"I'VE BEEN WAITING a long time for this." Jay Auden held a sinister-looking bowie knife up to the edge of my face, digging the tip into the skin just below my right eye.

"If you think Ralston is going to let you mar me before he gets paid, you're even more out of your mind than I thought," I said, pleased I kept the tremor out of my tone. Jay Auden was possibly the second most terrifying human I'd ever met. The first would be his brother—the ultimate sociopath.

"Do you think I give a shit what that old man wants?" He dug the knife deeper, and I felt warm blood trickle down my cheek.

"I think you only care about yourself."

"And revenge." He grinned, showing off perfectly white, straight teeth as he pressed the knife in deeper and sliced down.

White-hot pain shot like electricity through my cheek and I tried to jerk back, but the Duct tape holding me to the chair was too strong.

The door to the small cabin of the ship burst open, slamming against the metal wall. "Auden. What the fuck are you doing?" Ralston roared from the entry. "You're damaging the goods."

Damaging the goods. Not 'stop torturing the woman.' No, the goods. As if I was just a product to be bought and sold. My stomach lurched, and I struggled to not vomit. The reality of my situation came crashing down around me. I had no phone, no firearm, and I was bound to a wooden chair on a cargo ship headed for the other side of the world. The only hope I had was that the ship had yet to set sail.

Ralston stalked over to me, inspecting my wound. "Jesus. This is going to leave a scar." The director spun and backhanded Auden across the face, sending the man crashing into the metal wall. "I'll be taking the lost revenue out of your pay. Now get the fuck out of here and bring me back a first aid kit."

Auden stared up at him from the spot where he was sprawled on the floor. "That bitch killed my brother. I'll do whatever the fuck I want to her." He produced a handgun from his boot and aimed it straight at Ralston's head.

Ralston tentatively raised his hands. "Jesus, man. I'm not the enemy. We're both just trying to get paid. Relax. This is all just a misunderstanding."

Auden touched the edge of his lip, collecting blood on his fingertips. He stared at the bright red blood and then glared at Ralston. "You dared raise a hand to me. I told you when I started working with you I was a partner, not one of your hired hands to do your bitch work."

Ralston let out a nervous laugh. "Hey, hey. There's no need for the gun here. I'm sorry. I lost my cool. I was expecting this one to bring big cash, so I lost it for a second. It won't happen again."

Auden narrowed his eyes, studying Ralston for a long moment. Then he lowered the gun and pushed himself to his feet, rubbing the back of his head. "Do that again, and I won't hesitate to blow your fucking head off."

He wasn't bluffing either. The Auden brothers had zero conscience. I'd learned that the hard way.

Ralston nodded once and then moved toward the door, but just before he got there, he produced his own gun.

Auden was ready for him though, and kicked out, connecting with Ralston's knee. The larger man went down hard, knocking everything over, including Auden. The pair of them grappled, each landing awkward blows to the other as they fought to gain the upper hand.

I stared at the bowie knife now nestled near my foot. Auden had lost it while wrestling with Ralston. The only way it would do me any good is if I toppled my chair over. I wouldn't be able to reach it otherwise.

I glanced once more at the fight still battling in front of me. They were both in a fit of rage, and with any luck, they'd momentarily forgotten all about me.

Taking a deep breath, I threw all my momentum to the right, but only managed to tilt the chair slightly before it slammed back into place.

I noted Ralston's eyes flicker to me, but it cost him. Auden got the better of him with a blow straight to the throat that sent him into a coughing fit.

Shit!

If Auden ended him too fast, I'd never get out of here. I'd suffer for days on end before he decided to finish me off.

Luckily, Ralston was a professionally

trained killer and didn't let something as trivial as breathing stop him. He reached out and grabbed Auden around the throat, no doubt intending to crush his windpipe.

It was now or never. Using every last bit of strength I had, I threw myself to the right and landed with a hard thud on my shoulder. The shock of the blow knocked the air out of me, but I didn't let it slow me down. The knife was right there at my fingertips.

My fingers closed over the wooden handle just as Auden broke free from Ralston and the two once again lunged for each other, fists flying and grunts filling the small metal room.

"Please, God. Let this work," I whispered and pointed the knife toward the tape that was keeping my right hand strapped down. Luckily, there was just enough gap between my wrist and the arm of the chair that I was able to lodge the knife up against the tape. And because Auden was a freakin' psycho and had sharpened the knife to insane levels, the tape all but melted apart.

The commotion stopped, and I once again focused on Ralston and Auden. Ralston was lying on the floor, his face a bloody mess and one arm bent at an unnatural angle. It was highly unlikely the FBI director was breathing. Auden was standing over me, hatred streaming off him in waves.

This was it. I was done for. Without another thought, I thrust the knife as hard and fast as I could against the rest of the tape keeping me strapped to the chair. Fire burned up my arm, and I knew without a doubt, I'd just filleted myself. But it didn't matter. The tape had been cut enough that I at least had one arm free.

The one that held the bowie knife.

I met Auden's soulless eyes and in a voice I didn't even recognize, I said, "Your brother tried to rape me. And I shot him in the head for it. What do you think I'm going to do to you if you try to kill me?"

Uncontrollable rage consumed Jay. It was the same rage I'd seen rise up in his twin, Jared, on that horrid night when I'd tried to break up with him. Jay's face turned purple, and his muscles bunched as he closed his fists. He opened his mouth, but words wouldn't come out as his face scrunched up, making him appear deranged.

And when he threw himself at me, no doubt prepared to tear me limb from limb, I struck.

The knife slid right across Auden's Achilles

tendon.

A loud roar echoed through the small room as Auden fell to one knee, reaching for his ankle.

I took no chances and stabbed again, this time jabbing him in the thigh, aiming for his femoral artery.

"You bitch!" Auden cried and reached for me, but I swung at his hand, managing to connect with his wrist and palm. Blood was everywhere, dripping off him as he pulled back.

An eerie calm came over him as he backed up and studied me, his blood drops echoing in silence.

I sucked in a breath, trying to form a plan. He was too far away for me to use the knife now, and I was still mostly bound to the chair. If he went for his gun, I was done for.

"You're going to drop that knife now that you've had your fun."

I gripped it tighter. He'd have to crush my hand to get it away from me.

He laughed, the sound hollow and empty, as he hobbled awkwardly over to a small closet just to his left.

I scooted back and rammed into the wall. He was between me and the doorway, not that I could run even if I did manage to get to my feet. Not with me still strapped to the chair. I frantically cut at the tape binding my other arm, succeeding in slicing a few inches.

Auden reached into the storage closet and retrieved what looked like a giant, rusted pipe wrench. The way he was hefting it made it appear at least fifty pounds.

I tried to swallow as my eyes bugged out.

The weapon in my hand was not going to hold up to that monster.

"Drop the knife," he said again, his tone full of fury.

I couldn't bring myself to do it. If I did, I would be giving up, and I knew at that point I was a dead woman either way.

He glanced at the storage closet. "There are more horrors awaiting you in there. I like to be prepared. Drop the knife now or I'll use every single one of them on you until the last drop of blood has been drained from your pathetic body."

Fear coiled tightly in my chest, but that same thing, that same determination I'd grabbed hold of and clung to the night I'd survived his brother was right there at the surface, waiting for me. "Why don't you release me from this chair and then we can see who's really the stronger sex? Seems pretty weak and cowardly to have to tie up a girl just to get the upper hand, don't you think?"

"Stop!" he yelled. "I don't need to prove shit to you." He kicked Ralston's body with his injured foot, appearing to feel no pain. "I ended him with my bare hands. And I'll do the same to you."

"Bring it on," I taunted.

He lowered the wrench, but didn't drop it as he came nearer to me, once again limping heavily. "Do you think I'm an idiot?"

"I do," an angry male voice said from the doorway, followed by the ringing sound of a gunshot.

Wren. He'd found me.

A single bullet hit Auden in the left shoulder, sending him toppling forward. The wrench fell with a loud crack onto the floor just as Auden crashed into me and right on top of the knife, the lethal weapon spearing his chest.

He went completely limp, and I screamed, my world turning to chaos as I finally let the panic crawl its way in.

CHAPTER 12
WREN

It had been two weeks since the traumatic encounter with the FBI director and his partner, Jay Auden. Bella had been given a leave of absence, pending the investigation, and she'd spent all of that time with me at my family's Hidden Bayou Resort.

Fischer and his sister, who'd we'd found locked in another part of the ship, had gone back to Nashville to testify and to supply the FBI with more details on the human trafficking ring Ralston had been profiting from.

Ryker had called a week ago to inform us that Charlie's Little Darlings had indeed been engaging in forced pornography and had been put out of business, courtesy of the Dragons of Decatur. There'd been no word on which city official had been involved. Ryker assured us that we could be reasonably positive no more prints of Thea would be found floating about the greater New Orleans area.

All that was left to do now was to convince Bella she needed to stay. To be my mate.

It was early afternoon, and we were lying on my bed, the shades up as the sun spilled over us. Bella was curled on her side, facing away from me; a habit she'd picked up ever since that bastard Auden had sliced her face.

It didn't bother me. Nor did the scar on her forearm. Though I knew that if she ever did agree to be my mate, those scars would heal with the change.

I lightly ran my fingers over her bare shoulder. "My cousin Jace and his mate Skye are having a barbeque at their cabin tonight. Are you up for it?"

She was silent as she lay there, unmoving.

"Bella?" I craned my neck to see if she'd fallen asleep. No. She was wide awake, staring at the closet door. "You okay?"

She turned her head and met my eyes with a determined stare. Then she sat up and put a few inches distance between us. "What would you say we're doing here?"

I raised my eyebrows, startled by her question. "Here? I'd say we were considering an afternoon nap." Then I smiled, hoping to lighten the mood. "Unless you were hoping for something a little more... energetic."

She just stared at me. No smile. No smirk. Not even a roll of her eyes. We'd been intimate every night since she'd come to stay with me. At first, our lovemaking had been desperate; the kind that happens after people have gone through traumatic events. But then it gradually turned achingly tender.

Every night I craved showing her just how much I wanted her, needed her. And how it had all but ripped my wolf heart out when I'd thought I'd lost her so soon after finding her. Our nights were passionate, full of emotion and everything we hadn't been brave enough to say to each other.

"I mean us, Wren. I need to know what this is between us." She said the words with a quiet strength, void of judgment. But there was urgency there, and I had a feeling that our relationship hinged on whatever I said next.

There was no choice for me but to be honest. To lay the truth at her feet and let her decide.

I took her hand in mine and used my thumb to trace circles over her knuckles. "I can't speak to what you're feeling, but from where I'm sitting, Bell, I'm in. One hundred percent. I want you. All of you. In every way possible."

She sucked in a sharp breath and averted her eyes, staring at my blue comforter.

"Is that not what you wanted to hear?" My heart thudded against my ribcage. I'd blurted out everything I'd been trying to show her for the last two weeks. Surely my words couldn't have been that big a shock. I'd barely left her side. I hadn't even gone into work. My wolf hadn't let me.

"Every way?" she asked, her eyes filling with tears.

A sharp pain stabbed my heart as I wiped away one lone tear. I wanted her more than I ever thought possible, and the idea that she didn't feel the same gutted me. Ripped my insides to pieces, but I was lost to her. Couldn't give her up if I tried. "Oh, Bell, my gorgeous girl. You don't have to do anything you don't want to. If you don't want to be part of the pack, that's not a decision I'd force on you. You have to know that. I just want you by my side for as long as possible. You call the shots here."

She let out a watery laugh and gripped my hand, holding so tight that if I hadn't been a wolf, I was certain she'd have crushed a finger or two. "There are a few things about me you should know."

A chill crawled up the back of my neck at her words. But I nodded, determined to hear her out.

"I joined the FBI because I needed somewhere to belong. I don't have any family. Well I do, but we're estranged. Both of my parents are in prison."

I lightly squeezed her hand, lending her my support. "For what?"

Her face turned cold and determined. "I never talk about this, but I think you have a right to know. Jared Auden? The man who I dated and killed when he tried to rape me?"

I nodded again, though I got the feeling she was recapping the events for herself, rather than me.

"He worked for my parents, laundering money through a record store. That's how I met him, though I had no idea at the time he or my parents were involved in anything illegal. All I knew was they had invested in this indie record store and this cool older guy ran it. Only he wasn't cool, and neither were my parents. They dealt in high-end escorts, prostitution and drug smuggling. They were the bad guys. Did a lot of illegal stuff, but ultimately went to prison for fraud."

"Jesus," I whispered. "Your parents? That's awful." My family situation hadn't been a walk in the park, but it was never anything that torrid. Just a runaway mother and a drunk father. But the pack was strong. I'd never felt alone in my life.

"That's not the worst of it." She cast her

eyes down again and plucked at the blanket. "The night Jared tried to rape me, they were angry. Not because I'd been assaulted, but because I'd killed the guy who handled their money. They actually told the police I was lying." She choked on the word "lying" as a sob got caught in her throat.

My heart shattered right there, and I pulled her into my arms, holding her tight against my chest. Hatred for people I hadn't even known made me cold with quiet rage.

"The evidence said otherwise, of course," she said, when she got her breathing back under control. "Three months later they were indicted, and a year after that they both went to prison for a very long time."

I tightened my hold on her and kissed her temple. "And what did you do, love?"

"I worked my way through college and joined the FBI so I could be a part of something bigger than myself."

"That's admirable."

She nodded. "I guess. But it's not what I was looking for." Pulling away slightly, she glanced up at me. "It turns out I think I need a real family. One that I'm connected to in here." She pointed to her chest, right where her heart was. "I think I'd like to be a part of this." She waved her other hand around the room. "What you have with your brothers and their mates."

I stared at her finger still aimed at her heart. "I think I need you to spell it out for me, Bella." Raising my gaze to hers, I cupped her cheek with my hand. "Are you saying you want to be part of my pack, or are you saying you want to be my mate?"

"I'm saying I want both." She smiled into my eyes and curled her arms around my neck. "I want you and everything that comes with the privilege of being yours. But I also want, no need, for you to understand where I come from and why I need it so much. I want you to make the decision to take me, knowing it's not *just* you I need, but your family and your pack, too."

I let out the breath I'd been holding and dipped my head, claiming her lips, claiming her, making sure she knew who she belonged to. And when I finally let her go, I said, "As long as you understand that once I make you mine, once you become one of us, the pack comes first. I know you have your FBI job, but they aren't always on our side. And as I'm sure you know, we wolves often run into certain situations that—"

She held up her hand. "I'm leaving the FBI."

"You are? But you don't have to, you know. I'd never ask you to give that up if—"

"Stop." She chuckled. "I'm leaving. I don't want to be sent off to fight the bad guys. I want to be here, with you in New Orleans."

I eyed her, knowing she'd never in a million years be a house wife. She was entirely too independent. "Doing what?"

She shrugged. "I don't know. Maybe I'll open a business, or go into politics, or sell art at Jackson Square."

A smile pulled at my lips. "That's quite the eclectic list."

"I know," she said, smiling as she gently urged me down onto the bed. "But I never took the time to figure out what I really wanted to do. This time I will. But first," she raked her nails down my bare chest, "right now I know exactly what I want. And it's you."

I needed no other encouragement, and in one swift movement, I pulled her sundress over her head, leaving her entirely naked as she straddled me. I eyed her. "No undergarments?"

"I told you I knew what I wanted. Now make me yours."

I let out a low growl, gripped her hips, and flipped her over onto her back. Her eyes went soft as she watched me discard my pants and boxer briefs. "You're mine, Bella," I whispered into her ear as I nudged her legs apart to lie between them.

"I have been for a while." She lifted her legs and wrapped them around my hips. "Now, make it official, would you?"

"Gladly." And then I entered her and proceeded to take my sweet time, making her whimper with pleasure until finally, we both cried out right before I bit her, joining us as mates forever.

Sign up for Kenzie's newsletter at www.kenziecox.com to be notified of new releases. Do you prefer text messages? Sign up for text alerts! Just text SHIFTERSROCK to 24587 to register.

Book List:

Wolves of the Rising Sun

Jace

Aiden

Luc

Craved

Silas

Darien

Wren

Printed in Great Britain
by Amazon